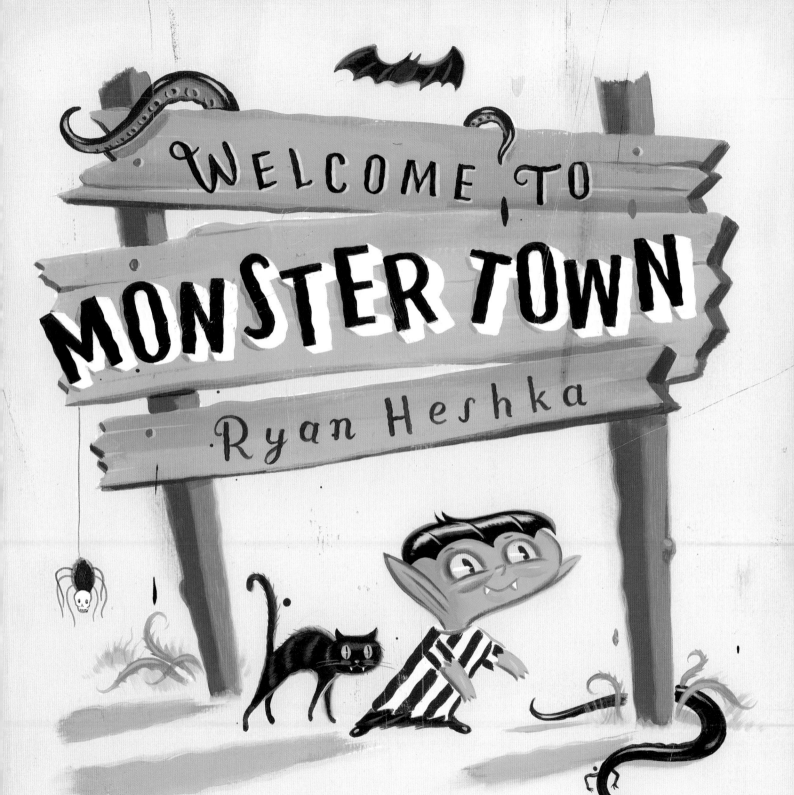

# WELCOME TO MONSTER TOWN

Ryan Heshka

Christy Ottaviano Books
Henry Holt and Company • New York

The sun sets on Monster Town . . .

The zombies are on their way to work.

The ghost writers
cover the news.

Postmaster Skeleton
delivers the monster mail.

The vampire bats work at the blood bank.

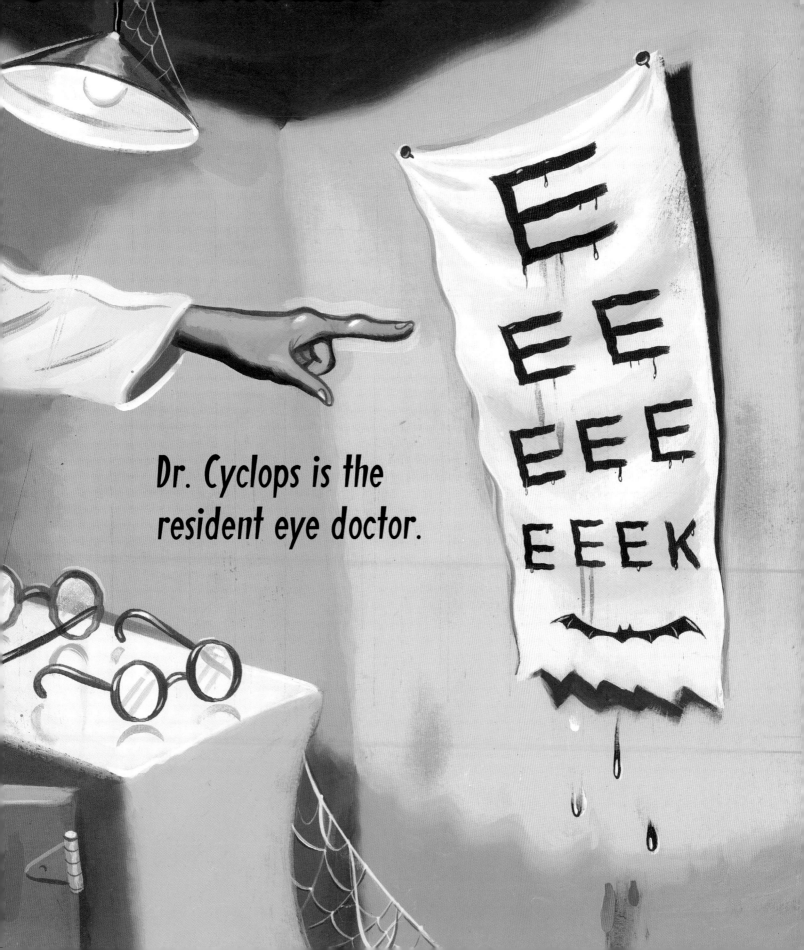

Dr. Cyclops is the resident eye doctor.

Dr. Mummy, the veterinarian,
takes good care of monster pets.

Wolfman Jacques gets ready to snip 'n' cut at the barbershop.

The Spider Brothers are
hardworking window cleaners.

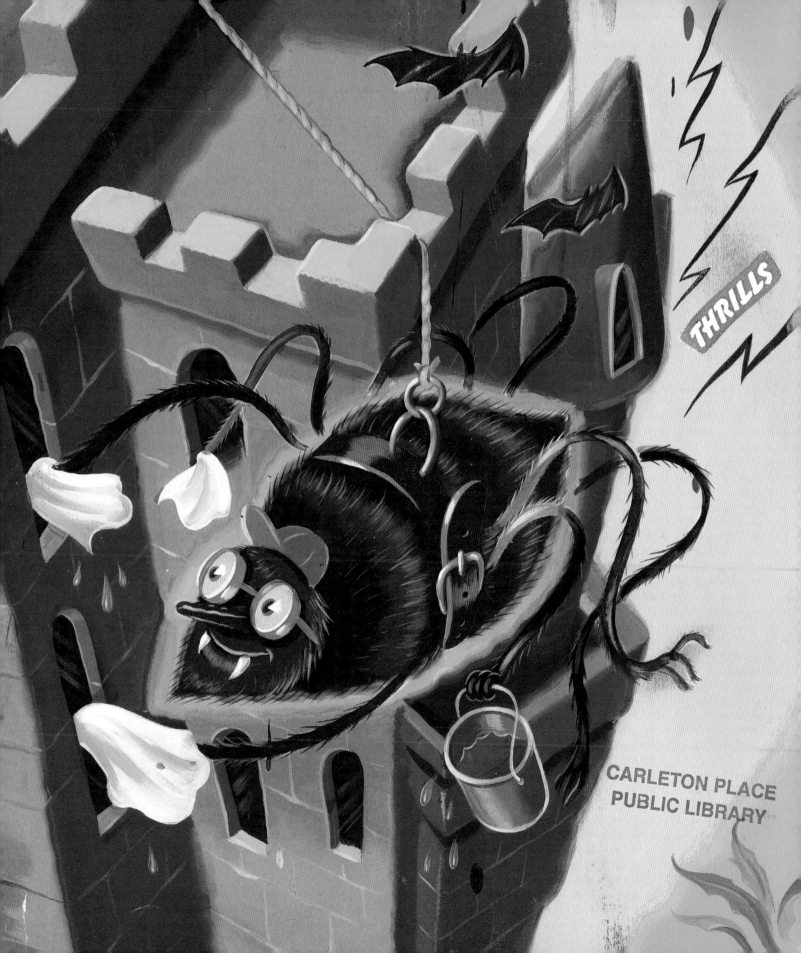

THRILLS

Giant Squid serves the best midnight brunch in town.

Frank N. Stein, master electrician,
appears shockingly good at his work.

And Captain Witch is always happy to fly United Scare Lines.

After a busy day in Monster Town,
the sun rises and it's time to sleep.

# To Tyler and Uncle Jodi,
## the original inhabitants of Monster Town

Thanks to Marinda Van't-Haaff, Lorne and Joan Heshka,
Tyler Heshka, Kate Larkworthy, Monte Beauchamp (BLAB!),
Kirsten Anderson, and Christy Ottaviano

Henry Holt and Company, LLC
Publishers since 1866
175 Fifth Avenue
New York, New York 10010
www.HenryHoltKids.com

Library of Congress Cataloging-in-Publication Data
Heshka, Ryan.
Welcome to Monster Town / by Ryan Heshka. — 1st ed.    p.   cm.
Simple text introduces the hardworking residents of Monster Town,
including Postmaster Skeleton and Frank N. Stein, an electrician.
"Christy Ottaviano Books."
ISBN 978-0-8050-8873-1
[1. Monsters—Fiction.]  I. Title.    PZ7.H43257Wel 2010    [E]—dc22    2009029315

First Edition—2010
Acrylic and collage on illustration board were used to create the illustrations for this book.
Printed in April 2010 in China by South China Printing Company Ltd.,
Dongguan City, Guangdong Province, on acid-free paper. ∞

1  3  5  7  9  10  8  6  4  2